LOST
IN PETER'S TOMB

Written by Dianne Ahern
Illustrated by Katherine Larson

AUNT DEE'S ATTIC

Adventures With Sister Philomena,
Special Agent to the Pope:
LOST IN PETER'S TOMB

Text © 2006 Dianne M. Ahern
Illustrations © 2006 Katherine Larson

A Book from Aunt Dee's Attic

Published by *Aunt Dee's Attic, Inc.*
415 Detroit Street, Suite 200
Ann Arbor, MI 48104

Printed and bound in Italy by Printer Trento

Library of Congress Control Number: 2005909126

ISBN 0-9679437-9-5

1 2 3 4 5 6 7 8 9 10

First Edition

www.auntdeesattic.com

*This book is dedicated to the memory of
Pope John Paul II.
God bless you, John Paul II, John Paul the Great.*

SPECIAL THANK YOU AND ACKNOWLEDGEMENTS

The office of The Patrons of the Arts in the Vatican Museums and its staff for opening the doors to the Vatican Museums, the Vatican Gardens, St. Peter's, and all the art, mystery and wonders therein.

Our friend and priest reviewer, Father Eric Weber, a graduate of the Pontifical Gregorian University, Rome, Italy.

The proofreaders, editors and reviewers who came to the aid of the author. Thank you Lisa Tucci, Josiah Shurtliff, Barbara Kelly, Shiobhan Kelly, Leo DiGiulio, Michelle Miner, Lauren and Kristin Bos.

The children who shaped the story, including Delaney and Riley Miner, Austin and Blake Witchie, and Lucy Gerstenschlager.

GOING TO ITALY

Riley lifts the shade on the big jet's window and looks out. He pokes his dad in the ribs to wake him up. "Hey, Dad, look out there!" Riley looks on in amazement.

"What's wrong with those clouds?" Riley asks. The morning sun is reflecting off the clouds, setting them ablaze in deep reds and hot pinks. Some of the clouds look like they have bolts of lightning zig-zag-ging through them, but the light stays lit and doesn't ZAP out like real lightning.

Sleepily, Riley's dad leans over and looks above his son's head to see out the window. "Oh!" he says. "Those aren't all clouds. Those high jagged edges and points you see are the tops of the Alps poking up through the clouds. Look over there where there aren't any clouds. You can see the craggy gray mountaintops with patches of snow. The sun's reflection off the snow and ice make the mountains look like they are on fire. How majestic!"

Opening the magazine from the seat pocket in front of him, Riley finds the section with a map of Europe.

He draws his finger along their current route that shows them crossing over the border of Switzerland and Austria, approaching Italy from the north.

"Is this where we are?" Riley asks his dad. "Why, yes it is," says his dad pleased that his son has figured out their route. "These are the Swiss Alps near the northern border of Italy. Soon we will follow this route that will take us over *Monte Bianco*, the highest mountain in northern Italy. Then we'll fly along the Mediterranean Sea coast. About half way down the west coast of Italy we will make a left turn and glide right into the Rome airport, our final destination."

"Delaney wake up! Look at the Alps!" Riley demands. He reaches around behind his seat and pokes his little sister.

"Mommy, look at the Alps!" says an excited Delaney as she stretches up to look out the window. "What are Alps?" questions the little girl trying to figure out what she's supposed to be seeing.

Delaney, Riley's younger sister, and their mom are seated behind Riley and their dad. They are on the last leg of their flight to Rome, Italy. It has been an over night journey and they have been dozing off-and-on for the last few hours. But now the anticipation of what lies ahead is starting to fill their thoughts.

Riley loves to travel and see new places. But this trip is a little different and he's not so sure he's going to like it. His parents are meeting with agricultural leaders in Europe this summer. Rather than leave Delaney and him at home with a nanny, his parents decided it would be good for the kids to spend some time with their Aunt Philomena. That would be fine if Aunt Philomena was a normal aunt. But their aunt is a nun and she lives in a convent in Grottaferrata, Italy, which is somewhere near Rome. What is a boy supposed to do in a boring old convent all summer? All that Riley can imagine is a whole summer with his little sister and a bunch of nuns going to church and praying all day. The uncertainty of it all makes him feel restless inside.

In the airport Riley helps his dad pull the family's luggage off the big moving belt and place it onto a pushcart. A man in military garb checks their passports and bags and then waves them through customs. He doesn't talk, he doesn't smile, he just sends them on with efficient authority.

"*Signore* from America!" shouts a uniformed limousine driver as the family exits the airport terminal. "Over here!" he waves and smiles. "My name is Massimo and I will drive you to the convent in

Grottaferrata." Eagerly and efficiently the driver loads the family's entire luggage into the trunk of the limousine.

Leaving the airport, they enter onto the *Autostrada*. Riley is quick to notice that traffic is heavy and moving very fast. The town names at the exits all end in 'o' or 'a' or 'i' or 'e' – and he knows that's an Italian way of spelling. Rather than Rome, it's called *Roma*.

The limousine driver follows signs that point the way to Grottaferrata. Soon the driver turns onto a local road which quickly becomes very narrow with barely enough room for two cars to pass.

The houses look much different than the houses back home. These houses have tile roofs and are either made of stones or tan and brown colored stucco. They look old. The windows have shutters and even though it is early afternoon, most of the shutters are closed. Riley wonders why that is. At home they rarely close shutters or drapes in the daytime--his mom likes a house full of light. What else will be different in Italy?

About a half-hour after leaving the *Autostrada* the limo pulls into a long drive with walls of tall slender cypress trees on each side. A sign mounted on stone pillars that frame a heavy iron gate reads, *Sisters of*

The houses look much different than the houses back home.

Saint Francis -- Missionaries of Charity. The gate barring the driveway is opened electronically after announcing who they are. Riley stretches to see what's at the end of the drive. It's a church. "Will this end up being an entire summer of going to church and praying?" he wonders to himself. Riley doesn't know what to make of it all and he slumps back into the seat.

Before reaching the church the limo turns left and stops in front of a three-story white washed stucco building with a statue in front. The statue is of a man with a wolf beside him and a bird sitting on his arm. "So this is what a convent looks like," says Riley under his breath. "What would my friends back home think if they knew about this?"

6

Getting out of the car Riley is overcome by the peacefulness of the place. Birds are chirping and the sun is very hot on his skin but the air seems cool. Palm trees sway in the breeze along side the regular trees. Palm trees? This is the first time he's seen real live palm trees.

"Come look over here," says Riley's dad who is standing alongside a stone wall at the edge of the parking lot.

Riley cannot believe his eyes. Miles and miles of rolling hills fan out in front of him. Off in a distance is a cream colored city. Nearer-in are villages skirted in green and a small blue lake.

"That's Rome way out there," says Riley's dad pointing to the cream colored city. "The seven hills of Rome! Between Rome and here are the towns of Frescati, Marino, and Castel Gondolfo. Castel Gondolfo is where the Pope spends his summer. Maybe if you're lucky you will catch a glimpse of him...that is if your aunt is allowed to leave the convent and take you and Delaney into the village."

Riley's eyes open wide. "What do you mean, 'IF she is allowed to leave the convent'?"

CONVENT LIFE

All of a sudden the convent's big wrought iron front doors burst open and his Aunt Philomena comes racing towards them. She is jumping for joy and shouting, "*Ciao, Ciao*! Welcome, welcome!"

Aunt Philomena smothers Riley and Delaney with hugs and kisses and entraps them in the flowing material of her habit. Delaney giggles and laughs with glee. Riley holds back and tries hard to not show any excitement. He's not sure how he should act.

Several other nuns all in white and black habits come to greet the travelers. They are all talking in Italian and Riley can't understand a thing. The nuns unload the luggage from the limo and take it into the convent. It looks like they have been waiting for them to arrive.

"I'm doomed," Riley thinks to himself. "I bet there isn't another boy within ten miles."

As they enter through the arching front door, Riley notices that the inside of the convent is very plain, orderly and cool even though it is very hot out-side in the sun. Despite the shuttered windows the place is sunshine bright. It is also very quiet, almost funeral home quiet. The nuns with the luggage scurry around. Then almost without making a sound they disappear. "Where did they all go?" he wonders. "They are sneaky and quiet like cats."

"The children and I will be staying in the guest quarters for the summer," Sister Philomena explains to Riley, Delaney and their parents. "The Reverend Mother and the other sisters decided the guest quarters would be more fitting. Because the children are young, and most undoubtedly because one of them is a boy, the Reverend Mother suggests, rather insists, that I be with them at all times. We'll have such a great time," she says swinging Delaney in the air like a rag doll then setting her down.

"Yea!" Shouts Delaney in total ecstasy. "I get to stay with Aunt Philomena!"

"We will make it work," says Sister Philomena looking at a long faced Riley. She tussles Riley's hair as a gesture of endearment. He just hates when people do that.

Looking around, Riley sees that the 'guest quarters' consist of two rooms. One is a bedroom that has three small beds separated by curtains, three rickety looking dressers and a sink with a mirror over it. The other room has two easy chairs, a lumpy looking

10

"Look at me, I'm a cocoon!"

couch and two desks with straight-backed chairs. A bathroom with a sign on the door that says 'WC' for 'water closet,' is across the hall from the rooms. The WC contains a bathtub, sink, toilet and three racks of towels.

There is no sign of a TV or computer or even a radio. "What kind of 'guest quarters' is this? It's more like a prison!" Riley thinks to himself. "This just will not work. I have to find a way out of here!"

Sister Philomena and Riley's mother chat non-stop while putting his and Delaney's things into the dressers. Delaney is snooping through everything like she usually does. She is always getting into stuff.

"Look at me, I'm a cocoon!" giggles Delaney as she wraps herself into one to the curtains that separates two of the beds.

A feeling of dread comes over Riley. No TV, no computer, no radio and no walls! He has to think and think fast.

So here's his plan.

It's almost dinnertime and Riley is quite sure his family will be going out to a fancy restaurant. After his parents have had a glass or two of wine and are relaxing, he'll break the news. He will not be staying in the convent, PERIOD! Delaney can stay there but he will not. Either they take him with them or send him back home.

Unbeknownst to Riley dinner plans had already been made. Riley's mom explains that the family will eat dinner in the convent with the sisters. The nuns have been looking forward to their visit and have prepared a special meal. Riley's mother has no intention of changing plans, and certainly will not disappoint the sisters who have gone to considerable trouble. Now Riley realizes he will not have the 'bargaining' time with his parents that he needs. Panic starts to fill his body.

Riley's heart sinks into his shoes as they enter the convent's dining room. The dining room looks like a poor parish's church hall. No frills! Uncomfortable looking wooden chairs are set around long wooden tables. Each table is set with a big pitcher of water, what appears to be a jug of wine, and baskets filled with bread and breadsticks. Riley feels trapped.

Then he realizes that the smell of food that floods the air is absolutely wonderful. He cannot think any more. He's confused. He is also very hungry.

The family sits among the sisters in the dining room. Reverend Mother leads them in saying the *Prayer Before Meals*. Riley's eyes start to sting with tears just thinking about an entire summer trapped in a convent with nothing to do but pray. Sure, they pray before meals at home and before they go to bed, and that's all right. But he's just sure that the nuns overdo it.

A cheerful short round-faced nun brings out plates of lettuce wedges with slices of tomatoes and cucumbers and hands out little pitchers of rich olive oil and vinegar. When everyone is finished eating the salad, huge platters of spaghetti with a light tomato sauce and grated cheese appear at the tables. Next come bowls of green beans and plates of some kind of fish. For desert they are offered fresh fruit and cheese and pastries that his mother

picked up at a local bakery before they arrived at the convent. It may not be the fancy fare Riley expected to have at a restaurant, but he does admit to himself that this food tastes awfully good.

After dinner Riley comes up with a new plan to flee the convent: Plan Number Two. Rather than argue with his parents tonight, he will just get up and be dressed and ready to go with them in the morning. He'll simply get into the car with them and refuse to get out. They will have to take him with them. Unfortunately, before Riley has a chance to figure out the details of this plan, his dad delivers some really bad news.

"The limousine driver heard on the radio that the Italian transportation workers are going on strike tomorrow. This happens all to often in Italy when the government workers are displeased about something. Anyway, all air flights, buses and trains departing after 9 AM in the morning have been cancelled for at least one day. This means your mother and I need to leave tonight," says Riley's dad. "We just have to be in Paris by noon tomorrow. We have no choice."

"You don't understand. I cannot stay here. There is no TV. There are no video games. There is nothing! There is no where to go! It's a convent!" Riley pleads to his father and mother as they prepare to leave.

Riley is sure his heart will break.

"Give it a couple weeks, Riley," says his mother encouragingly. "If you cannot adjust within two weeks we will arrange for you to fly home and stay with your friend Maria and her family. But you have to give it at least two weeks."

Riley is sure his heart will break. It has been a very long day and he feels lost and alone...and now without a plan! He feels like crying but knows that he shouldn't. That would show weakness and he wants to be strong – he has to be tough.

He looks for Delaney and spots her being all chitty-chatty and laughing with some of the nuns. "Oh, great," he thinks, "making friends with the enemy. She's no help."

After their parents leave Sister Philomena helps Delaney get ready for bed. Riley uses the WC to put on his pajamas. He piles his clothes and dirty towels on the floor as a means of protest. But he is just too tired to put up any more of a stink. Tomorrow he will come up with Plan Number Three. That's for sure!

In total exhaustion he crawls into bed and buries himself between the down comforter and the feather bed mattress. "Well, at least this bed is comfortable," he thinks to himself as he falls fast asleep.

GETTING THE CALL

Sister Philomena throws open the windows and shutters to the guest quarter's bedroom. Sun light and the fresh morning air fill the room.

"Children, wake up, wake up!" Sister Philomena paces back and forth between Delaney's and Riley's beds gently shaking them. The children just arrived yesterday and they have to be tired from their long trip. She had planned to let them sleep-in while she rearranged the guest quarters to give Riley a little more privacy.

"We have to go into the city, to Rome. Get up and get dressed as fast as you can. It's very important. I have to meet with the Holy Father. He thinks there is an intruder sneaking around the Vatican."

"What?" questions Riley, rubbing the sleep out of his eyes. "Whose father? What intruder?"

"I want my mommy," says Delaney in a very quiet and slightly quivering voice.

"Oh, Delaney, we don't have time for that now. The Holy Father has called," says Sister Philomena.

"I thought your boss was the Reverend Mother.

What's a Holy Father?" asks Riley. He frowns as he realizes he's in a convent.

"It's *il Papa*, the Pope," explains their aunt. "And I do not like to keep him waiting. He is sending his car for us. Reverend Mother only agreed to let you stay here if I supervised you at all times. Therefore you have to come with me. I did not anticipate the Pope calling this soon. *Oh, Dio Mio! Dio misericordioso.*"

"What?" asks Riley frowning at his aunt.

"Oh, it's just a prayer. I asked God to help us, to have mercy on us and to get you up and moving." Sister Philomena gives Riley a push to get him out of bed.

Reluctantly Riley gets up and pulls on the clothes he wore all day yesterday. They are wrinkled but he doesn't care. Sister Philomena fusses with Delaney to brush her hair. When all the tangles are gone she helps Delaney with her dress and cute little sandals. Satisfied that they look somewhat presentable Sister leads the children to the waiting car.

On the way Sister Philomena grabs three crusty buns, some sliced cheese, apples, juice boxes and bottled water from the nuns' dining room — a good breakfast by Italian standards. Once in the car, Sister begins preparing the children for their approaching visit with the Pope.

Reluctantly Riley gets up and pulls on the clothes he wore all day yesterday.

"We are going to see the Pope. No one outside the Vatican and the Italian police, except of course the Reverend Mother, knows that I work for the Pope. In particular, your parents do not know."

"Do you mean the real Pope?" questions Riley. "The one that heads up the Catholic Church?" Riley has studied about the Pope and the Holy See in his religion class. The Pope is the most important person in the entire world, by his estimation anyway. He cannot believe his aunt knows the Pope, much less works for him.

"One in the same," says Sister Philomena. "Now when we get there please be a perfect lady and gentleman. Use your very best manners and do not talk unless you are spoken to first. Do you understand, Delaney?" Of the two children Sister Philomena knows that Delaney is the least pre-dictable. Not only because of her age but also because she is what her mother calls a 'free spirit.'

"When the three of us are together you may call me Sister or Aunt or *Zia* Philomena – whatever you want. By the way, *Zia* is Italian for aunt. However when we are with the Pope, you must call me *Sorella* or Sister Philomena. *Sorella* is Italian for Sister. That is what the Pope calls me. *Capito*? I mean, do you understand?"

The rest of the drive was spent talking about manners, how to address the Holy Father and how to kiss his ring. Luckily these children have been exposed to the finer things in life and are well mannered.

Their breakfast of bread, fruit, juice and cheese is eaten in relative quiet. Sister prays that the children won't spill the food and drink all over themselves and the Pope's car.

"At home we eat doughnuts for breakfast," Delaney informs Sister Philomena. "Not dry bread," sighs the little girl as she plops the half eaten, ordinary bun on Sister's lap.

Sister Philomena laughs at this as she wipes Delaney's smudged face with the hem of her habit. She makes two mental notes: #1 always bring a wet towel when travelling with children, and #2 find a place in Rome to buy doughnuts.

MEETING THE POPE

Rome traffic is bumper to bumper with all makes and models of compact cars and what seem like hundreds of people on motorbikes and motor scooters. Horns honk and sirens blare.

"Yikes!" Riley and Delaney flinch as the bikes and scooters come right up to the sides of their big black car. Riley is amazed to see how the bikes stop just in time to avoid a collision.

"This place is crazy! I've never been anywhere like this!" says Riley.

Riley and Delaney are all eyes as they try to take in all the sites. Ancient ruins side-by-side with modern buildings. Crowded Rome sidewalks filled with people – open-air markets next to cafes next to small clothing stores next to bakeries – it's all so busy.

"That's the Tiber River," points out Sister Philomena as they come upon a winding river with shade trees along the banks. "It runs through the center of Rome. Vatican City, where the Pope lives, is just up here a little way."

"Wow," exclaims Riley. "What's that over there?"

He has almost lost his 'attitude' and forgotten his
plan to flee.

"You mean that big castle-like building with an
angel on top?" asks Sister Philomena. "That is the
Castel Sant'Angelo. A crazy Roman emperor built it a
long time ago. Many years later some Popes took it
over and used it as a hideaway. Today it's a museum."

"Who are they and what are they doing?" questions Delaney with a puzzled look on her face. The
empty eyes of the bigger-than-life statues that line
each side of the bridge over the Tiber stare down at
the little girl.

"Those are statues of angels," explains Sister
Philomena. "They were placed there hundreds of
years ago by a man named Bernini." Delaney frowns
and stares back at the statues. She always thought
angels were teeny-tiny – these angels look like giants.
Fortunately the trip to the city and all the new sights
has stolen Delaney's attention and she is no longer
asking for her mother.

Riley stretches to look over the front seat of their
car to see what's up ahead. As they turn onto a broad
boulevard, called *Via della Conciliazione*, St. Peter's
Basilica, with its huge dome, comes into view. In
front of the basilica is the area called *Piazza San Pietro*,

or St. Peter's
Square. Huge
columns on
each side flank
the square and
basilica. Above
the front of the
basilica and over
the columns are
even more statues.

"Is that where
we are going?
Why are those
statues up there?
Who are they?
What's that building?"
questions Riley.

"That is the
famous St. Peter's Basilica.
We're at the Vatican.
Those statues are of
Jesus, the Apostles,
the Church
fathers
and other
saints," says Sister
Philomena.

The car zips past the front of the Basilica and through a side gate. Two men dressed in strange red, blue and gold striped suits with puffy pants stand guard at the gate. Their hats look like helmets left over from some ancient war and they hold long shafted spears in their hands.

"Who are they?" asks Riley turning around to look out the back window as they drive past the guards. He doesn't know if he is entering the Vatican or some kind of fantasyland.

"They're the Swiss Guard, members of the Vatican security force. They protect the Pope," says Sister Philomena.

"So what do they do? Chase the bad guys away with those skinny spears," responds a sarcastic Riley. Well, maybe his 'attitude' isn't completely gone.

The car accelerates through the gate and around the back of the huge Basilica. It comes to an abrupt stop in a small interior court. Two more men in striped suits come up to the car. One opens the door and the other helps them out.

Riley and Delaney feel like they are standing in the center of a giant stone forest. Gray granite walls of the ancient buildings reach to the sky on all four sides. High above they can see a square of the morning sunlight.

Delaney grabs Riley's hand and points to what looks like a stone monster sitting in the shadow by the doorway. "What is that? Does it bite?" Turning around and looking up, "Eek! Will they jump?" Very mean looking stone figures guard the ancient doorway and perch over the windows. Some look like angels but others look like monsters and devils.

Sister Philomena chuckles. "Those are called gargoyles. They're just stone carvings and cannot hurt you. I agree, they are pretty scary looking." She reaches out and takes the little girl's other hand.

Riley has the feeling you get when you are in some place where you are not supposed to be. He's

having a hard time believing his aunt really knows anyone here, especially the Pope.

Then, like thieves in the night, a Swiss Guard rushes them through the door and up seemingly endless flights of wide marble stairs. Breathless, they reach the top floor. The landing area has a very high ceiling. Riley can see huge wooden double doors at the opposite end of this grand foyer and wonders what's behind them.

"Look, somebody drew pictures all over the walls," observes Delaney. "And on the ceiling too." Looking up at the ceiling and spinning around to take it all in, she stumbles and begins to fall. Hurtling forward she turns and lands on her bottom just as the big double doors open. On the other side is a man in a long white cassock with a cinch around his waist and a little white cap on his head. Sister Philomena nearly faints dead-away as Delaney, now plopped at the foot of the Pope, looks up and simply says, "Hi, I'm Delaney. Who are you?"

Riley panics and tries to hide behind his aunt as he realizes that this man is in fact the Pope.

"Your Holiness, I am so sorry," gasps Sister Philomena not knowing what to do first: pick up Delaney, kneel and kiss the Pope's ring, or just turn and run away as fast as she can.

Very mean looking stone figures guard the ancient doorway.

"Not to worry," says the Pope as he stoops to help Delaney get up.

"Not to worry," says the Pope as he stoops to help Delaney get up. "I am the Pope."

"She's my aunt," says Delaney pointing to her now red-faced aunt. "I can call her Aunt Philomena most of the time, but I have to call her *Sorella* or Sister Philomena when you are around."

"I see," chuckles the Pope. "And who are you," he asks leaning around to see who is hiding behind Sister Philomena.

"Your Holiness, this is my nephew Riley," says Sister Philomena as she drags him from behind her. "And you just met my niece, his sister, Delaney."

Sister Philomena first, followed by Riley and then Delaney, bows to the Holy Father and bends to kiss his ring. This is the greeting they had practiced in the car.

The Pope escorts them into his private study. The children are captivated by the room's tall stained glass windows and, like the grand hallway, paintings on the walls and ceiling.

A huge table that looks like it's a million years old sits in the center of the room. The Pope invites them to have a seat. Delaney and Riley nearly disappear as they sink into two of the big chairs set around the table.

Riley eavesdrops on the conversation between

the Pope and his aunt. They are talking about a suspected intruder.

"As I was telling you over the telephone, I am sure there is an intruder, a sneak, roaming around the inside of the Vatican," says the Pope. "Sometimes I even suspect there is somebody lurking in and around my apartment in the Apostolic Palace."

"But haven't the Swiss Guard made a thorough search?" asks Sister Philomena.

"Yes, but they have found nothing. That's why I need your assistance. It almost seems spirit-like sometimes," explains the Pope.

"You don't mean spirit, like ghost, do you?" asks Sister Philomena.

The Pope shrugs his shoulders and raises his eyebrows. "I know it is not a ghost. But it certainly is ghost-like."

Riley wonders, "Who would ever believe this? His aunt is talking with the Pope, and the Pope is asking his aunt for help on an investigation!"

After only a few minutes, Delaney starts
fidgeting and gets up on her knees to see the top of
the table. She helps herself to a pen and piece of
paper and starts to draw on it. Sister Philomena looks
on in horror. She feels totally inadequate in handling
children. Next time she will have to remember to
bring some toys or books along to keep the children
busy – mental note #3!

Riley frowns at his sister and tries to take the
pen and paper away.

"No! Mine!" bellows the little girl holding on
tight to her paper until it rips. "I want to make a
picture for the Pope's wall!"

"*Sorella* Philomena, why don't we continue our
discussion outside? I think the children would
enjoy the Vatican Gardens. They can run
freely and explore. That's what children like
to do. You look like you could use a walk
also," offers the Pope.

"Miss Delaney. You may finish
my picture later" says the Pope showing his guests to the door.

VATICAN GARDENS

Riley and Delaney can see why the Pope calls this place a palace. Paintings, statues and tapestries line the long hallway that leads to still another grand marble staircase.

Sister Philomena gasps as Delaney starts running down the stairs. Her footsteps on the marble steps echo through the huge open stairwell. Down and down she goes. Then she turns and runs back up the stairs. *Tip, tap! Tip, tap! Tip, tap!*

"Aren't there any elevators in this place?" Delaney asks breathlessly.

"Well there are a few that have been added recently," explains the Pope. "However this Apostolic Palace was built over 500 years ago and they did not have elevators back then. Myself, I rather prefer using the stairs. It's good exercise."

Riley grabs his sister to calm her down. "Slow down and act like a lady," he whispers.

At the bottom of the stairs they enter yet another very long hallway. They walk for what seems like forever and finally end up at a door with a sign that says *Giardini Vaticani.* Riley looks at the words and sounds them out. "I bet *giardini* means gardens in Italian. And *Vaticani*? – that has to mean Vatican. This is the door to the Vatican Gardens!" he proclaims proudly.

"That's right! Where did you learn Italian?" teases the Pope.

Riley smiles, then looks over to his aunt. She winks at him. He is starting to think that just maybe this visit with his aunt may not be so horrible after all. Riley remembers his dad saying that perhaps he could catch a glimpse of the Pope if they went to his summer residence in Castel Gondolfo. Well here he is talking to the Pope in the Vatican! His dad will never believe this, not in a million years.

The Pope, Sister Philomena and the two children walk out into the beautiful garden. The sunshine is so bright that it seems to make the colors of the grass, shrubs, trees and flowers come alive. The air is warm from the sun, but fresh and cool all at the same time.

Two more men in striped suits are standing guard at the archway where they enter the gardens. The guards click their heels and hold their spears at attention. Riley and Delaney snap back in surprise.

Taking a closer look, Riley realizes that the guards have gadgets like radios or cell phones on their belts. Maybe they spear the bad guys, then call for help.

A third guard appears from out of nowhere and salutes the Pope. The Pope smiles and gives a little wave of the hand. Then the guard bows toward Sister Philomena and the kids, touching the tip of his beret. "This is so cool it's frightening," thinks Riley.

"Those are my Swiss Guards," says the Pope. "They are part of the security force that guards the Vatican and protects me. Those striped suits, their uniforms, are modeled after uniforms the guards wore in the beginning of the 16th century. That's when the Swiss Guard began protecting the Popes."

"Have there been a lot of Popes?" asks Riley.

"There have been around 265," says the Pope. "Ever since the time of Christ's death and resurrection, there has been a Pope as the head of the Catholic Church. St. Peter was the first. Do you know about St. Peter?" asks the Pope.

"A little," says Riley. "We talked about him in my religion class. Ms. Kelly, my teacher, showed us pictures of Jesus and the Apostles at the Last Supper. I think Peter was at the Last Supper."

"Indeed he was," answers the Pope.

"How come Jesus picked Peter?" asks Riley.

"No one but God knows for sure," answers the Pope. "But I believe that Jesus looked into the soul of Peter and knew that he would be a good leader for His Church here on earth. Peter was a fisherman just trying to make a living when Jesus called him. Peter and his brother, Andrew, were tending their fishing nets. Jesus had borrowed their boat to sit in while He preached to the people on the shore. Afterward, Jesus singled out Peter and Andrew and said to them, *'come after me, and I will make you fishers of men' (Mt 4:19).* Peter and Andrew left everything behind and followed Jesus.

"The Gospel writers often put Peter close to Jesus when important things were happening. Peter

was there at the Transfiguration (Mk 9:2ff), the raising of Jairus' daughter from the dead as well as when the woman was cured by touching the hem of Jesus' robe (Lk 8:40-56), and at the Agony in the Garden (Mk 14:32-33), just to mention a few. Peter was also the first Apostle to enter the tomb after Jesus rose from the dead (Lk 24:12), and the first to see Jesus after His resurrection (1 Cor 15:5).

"Peter was the first to acknowledge Jesus' divinity and to proclaim Him *'the Messiah, the Son of the living God'* (Mt 16:16). In return, the Lord replied, *'And so I say to you, you are Peter, and upon this rock I will build my church, and the gates of the netherworld shall not prevail against it'* (Mt. 16:18). Jesus then said, *'I will give you the keys of the kingdom of heaven. Whatever you bind on earth shall be bound in heaven; and whatever you loose on each shall be loosed in heaven'* (Mt 16:19).

"The keys became the symbol associated with Peter and of the Papacy."

The Pope takes his rosary out of his pocket to show them. It has a Vatican seal right in the middle. "Look, wherever you see the emblem of the Vatican you will see the crossed keys – one silver and one gold. That represents Jesus giving the keys to Peter to give him authority over the Church."

"Children, run along and enjoy yourselves. Just stay within the Vatican walls," says the Pope.

"They are safe here," the Pope tells Sister Philomena. "The Swiss Guards are all around and will keep an eye on them. Now, you and I can talk."

"Who's this?" shouts Riley. He and Delaney have run on ahead and discovered a statue of a man set under some trees.

"How come he has chains hanging on him?" asks Delaney tracing the circle of chain with her fingers. She has climbed up on the lap of the statue to get a better look.

"That is a statue of St. Peter," states the Pope.

"But why is he chained?" demands Delaney.

"That's a part of Peter's story that I didn't quite get to. You should know that in the time when Jesus and Peter lived, about 2000 years ago, the Romans did not like the followers of Jesus, the Christians. In fact they would persecute the Christians and kill them. Sometimes they even threw them to the lions in the Coliseum.

"After Jesus' death and resurrection, the Romans tried even harder to stop Peter and the other Apostles from spreading Christianity. This one time they captured Peter, put him in chains, and threw him in a dark, dank underground prison. This statue shows Peter's despair over being imprisoned.

"But putting Peter in prison didn't work. With

God's help, Peter was able to shed the chains, walk out of prison, and continue his ministry. Not far from here is a church where the actual chains that held Peter prisoner are on display. The church is called *Chiesa di San Pietro in Vincoli*. That means Church of St. Peter in Chains."

"For real?" questions Riley.

"For real!" says the Pope. "Perhaps your aunt will take you there some day. Now run along and see what else you can find. Your aunt and I are right behind you."

"Let's go this way," says Delaney as she runs up a hill then down. They pass other statues, fountains, grottos, and come upon a huge pond. They stop at the pond to take a good look. In and around the pond are what look like moss covered monsters with water spurting out of their mouths.

43

Looking into the pond they see something drift across the water
like a dark cloud.

"Kind of creepy for a Holy place," Riley says to no one in particular. Delaney is leaning over the edge of the pond's rim trying to catch a gold fish. Riley grabs her by the hem of her dress and stops her just before she topples into the water.

Looking into the pond they see something drift across the water like a dark cloud. A cold chill runs down Riley's back. He looks up and realizes the source of the dark cloud is actually the reflection of a man dressed in black passing by the pond.

"Hold on, Delaney," he whispers. "I just saw a really strange looking guy over there behind the pond." Riley points out the dark figure with a hood over his head. "Look, he's pacing back and forth -- back and forth." The figure stops and peers into the green water. Then he turns and, seeing the children, pulls the hood over his face and slinks away.

"Could that be the Pope's intruder? It certainly looks like a spirit, an evil spirit!" says Riley.

"I think it looks like the boogeyman," whispers Delaney.

"There's no such thing as a boogeyman," Riley corrects his sister. Feeling shy and too embarrassed to tell his aunt about this, Riley decides to ignore the sighting. Maybe it's just his imagination.

"Come over here, Riley. Let's try to find the other end," pleads Delaney. She has just discovered a garden with hedges trimmed in the shape of a giant puzzle.

Halfway through the puzzle-like garden Delaney spots a white cat, her favorite animal.

The cat turns and runs away from her. Delaney runs after it and watches as the cat disappears into a big hole. The hole blends into the side of the hill and would have been missed if it weren't for the cat.

"Here, kitty, kitty," she calls.

Riley saw the cat too, and decides to help Delaney look for it.

They kneel down and peak inside the hole where they saw the cat disappear. Slimy green moss covers the stone steps that lead down into the hole. "I think the kitty is in there," Delaney points down the hole. "Let's go find it."

Riley takes Delaney by the hand and they cautiously take the first step into the hole. They see something move. It must be the cat. They take another step, carefully, then another step, deeper into the dark hole.

Halfway through the puzzle-like garden Delaney spots a white cat.

ST. PETER'S TOMB

The children begin to slide and tumble down through the cave-like hole in the ground. The light goes from sunny bright, to muddy yellow, to emerald green, and then black. The passage narrows and smells like dirt -- very old dirt.

Thump, thump. The two hit bottom.

Looking up, they can no longer see daylight. It's pitch dark. Delaney starts to panic. "Riley, where are we?" she cries.

"I don't know," he says, frantically reaching out to find his sister's hand. "But you can bet Aunt Philomena is going to go crazy if we disappear. Let's try to stand up."

The children, hanging onto each other for dear life, struggle to stand up. Stepping forward in the dark, dim lights flicker-on. "We must have triggered some motion sensor lights," observes Riley. "But where are we?"

"This looks like an underground village," says Delaney. "But it's so little."

They find themselves looking down a dim, dank,

miniature street with damp brick walls on both sides and dirt above them. The doorways and windows are small and low, not much taller than Riley. They take a few steps forward.

"Look in this room. See the little stone boxes and holes in the floor, and little windows. There's a broken statue and vase over there. But why is it here, underground?"

Delaney lets go of Riley's hand and carefully steps into the little room. She finds a small stone box and sits on it. Wide-eyed, she looks around. Her knees are shaking and she is very scared.

Off in the corner she sees a shadow move. Is it the cat?

Riley sees it too. "Maybe it's the cat," they think, "but it's a pretty big shadow for a cat. What if it's the Pope's intruder!?" Frightened, Riley grabs Delaney's hand and pulls her out of the little room and down the dwarfish alleyway. They try to run but the dirt floor is uneven and their legs are trembling. The dim light illuminates narrow passages and steps leading away from the main corridor, but they do not see any EXIT signs.

"There has to be a way out," says Riley. Fear and panic ring in his ears.

At the next bend they see the shadow again. Riley decides it's too big for a cat's shadow. It's either a

Off in the corner she sees a shadow move.

ghost or the intruder or . . . or . . . what else could it be?

"There are no such things as ghosts," Riley says, anticipating his little sister's fear. Reassuring himself, he repeats again, "there are no such things as ghosts."

Another turn, and another turn. Are they going up or going down? They cannot tell. This is the most scared Riley has ever been. "Let's crawl through here. I think I see more light on the other side."

They crawl into a small space toward a brighter light. Riley feels his way along on his hands and knees. Suddenly his hand bumps into something. It feels and looks like a small plastic box. Then his knee strikes another box, this one a little bigger. And then another small box. He picks this one up and shakes it. It rattles. What in the world?

Delaney, sensing his fear, begins to cry.

"What are you doing in there?" comes a man's voice. "Don't move another inch."

The shadow crosses in front of them again. Delaney begins to cry louder, then she begins to scream.

"Now don't cry and please don't scream. You could wake the dead," says the voice. "Just crawl back out, nice and slow."

It's the shadow talking. Is it really a ghost after all? Riley can feel his heart beating so hard in his chest that his ears feel clogged.

The shadow moves again. Riley turns around to get away from the shadow and finds himself facing a Swiss Guard. It is the same guard who saluted the Pope when they entered the Vatican Gardens.

"Come back out. Be careful not to disturb anything. You are in 'The Tomb'," says the guard.

Very carefully, Delaney and Riley back out of the tiny passageway. Delaney is now too scared to scream or cry.

The guard takes his flashlight and shines it on their clothes, hands and faces. "You're OK. You don't have much dirt on you," he says and brushes their hair with his hand. He takes his handkerchief and wipes Delaney's tear and dirt-streaked face. "You're a brave little girl."

"Did you move those boxes in the tomb?" the guard asks.

"Tomb?" What does he mean, questions Riley.

"Boxes? Yeah, I touched them. I shook one but didn't open it," says Riley. "Why? What's in them?"

"Those boxes contain the bones of St. Peter," says the Guard. "This is his tomb. He was buried here in the dirt nearly 2000 years ago."

"Huh?" says Riley. "You mean St. Peter, Jesus' Apostle, the first Pope? Those boxes I shook contain his bones?!"

"Are we in big trouble?" askes Riley.

"That's right. You are not allowed to be in here unless you have special permission from the Vatican Excavations Office. This is a very holy place and very few people are permitted to visit Peter's tomb."

"Are we in big trouble?" asks Riley. "We were just playing. We didn't mean to . . . to . . . they told us to run around and explore things. I don't even want to be here!"

"I know, I know," says the Swiss Guard. "Just calm down. The Holy Father asked me to follow you. I never expected that you would find your way in here."

"We were following the kitty," says Delaney. "I think its in one of the little rooms back there."

"Oh, that cat. Tarsus is his name," says the Swiss Guard. "Tarsus is the Pope's cat. It hangs out in here sometimes. Maybe that explains why there are never any mice in the scavi."

"What's the scavi?" asks Riley.

"*Como si dice*, in English? How do you say it in English?" the Swiss Guard questions himself. "Scavi means a digging or excavation. This underground digging is uncovering a burial ground or cemetery. It was covered up with dirt hundreds, no thousands of years ago. It was only discovered in the last century."

"There's dead people in here?" shrikes Delaney.

"*Si!* I mean 'yes'," says the Swiss Guard. "The

55

little rooms back there where you were looking around contain special burial chambers for the early Christians, some Jews, and a few Romans. That stone box you were sitting on actually contains the bones of someone who died in 30 BC; that's 30 years before the birth of Jesus."

Delaney's eyes pop open. "Dead people's bones are in that stone box?"

"Yes, but they cannot hurt you," laughs the Swiss Guard. He goes on explaining, "Those rooms are small because it cost a lot of money to bury people in these sarcophogi or stone coffins back then. But the surviving relatives wanted safe and secure burial places and places that were big enough for the family to visit from time to time. People who used these burial chambers believed in heaven and that people would rise from the dead on judgment day. The living family and friends would drop food and wine through those holes in the floor to ensure the dead would have something to sustain them on their journey to the next life."

"I think I would like to get out of this place. My aunt is up there with the Pope," says Riley pointing up. "Can you help us find them?"

"Sure. The Holy Father wanted me to keep an
eye on you while he and Sister Philomena were
working on some special investigation. We did not
expect you to get into St. Peter's tomb! Come, I will
lead you out. Then I will make a call to let them
know you are alright."

"You know my Aunt Philomena?" asks Riley.

"Oh yes, she is a very special lady. All the Swiss
Guards, as well as a lot of the *Polizia* and *Carabinieri,*
know and respect her."

"The who?" asks Riley in amazement.

"The *Polizia* are the local police and the
Carabinieri are federal police agents. We all know and
respect Sister Philomena because she is a wonderful
detective and crime specialist," says the Swiss Guard.
"The Pope respects her and relies on her services to
help him in special circumstances.

"Please, call me Capitano Leo. That's my rank
and name.

"Come on you two, let's get out of here."
Delaney grabs hold of Capitano Leo's hand to be led
out of St. Peter's Tomb. Riley is right at their heels.

PIAZZA SAN PIETRO

"**H**ave you been to Rome or the Vatican or St. Peter's Basilica before?" Capitano Leo asks Riley and Delaney as he leads them through the dark winding passageway going away from St. Peter's tomb.

"No. Our parents travel a lot, but Delaney and I always have to stay home. That is until now. This time Mom and Dad left us with our aunt. She lives in a convent," Riley says rather sheepishly.

"Don't worry," says Capitano Leo, sensing Riley's embarrassment over his living situation. "Sister Philomena is a wonderful person and I'm sure she will provide you with lots of adventure this summer. In fact, I guarantee it! This way now, we are almost out."

Suddenly a rush of fresh air hits them as Capitano Leo opens the door to exit the scavi. Finally, daylight and warm, dry air.

"Would you like to walk through the Basilica of Saint Peter on our way to meet the Holy Father and your aunt, Sister Philomena? It is a very holy place. Millions and millions of people come to visit this basilica every year."

"I guess so," says Riley. He's a little confused, but mostly he's glad to be in the daylight again.

Walking back through the gates where they drove

through earlier in the morning, the Swiss Guards smile and salute the Capitano and children. One guard picks up his radio and speaks into it. Riley realizes they are with someone who is very important.

All of a sudden Riley realizes they are standing in the middle of the famous St. Peter's Square, or

Piazza San Pietro as it is called in Italian.

"Pigeons!" shouts Delaney as she runs to, and then scatters a flock of pigeons resting and cooing near a big fountain. Delaney runs up to a little boy about her age, and they take turns chasing the birds. It's like the pigeons know it's a game and continue to

come back to tease Delaney and her new friend, only
to be chased away again.

For Riley, it feels as if he is standing in the middle of a giant fortress. He feels protected and safe, yet
open and free. A sense of awe and greatness comes
over him. This must be why they call it a 'holy place'.
It's kind of like being inside a prayer. Silently he
recites the *Our Father*.

"A little souvenir for the children?" asks a ven-
dor carrying a tray filled with medals, little statues,
beads, and cards.

"*Certamente,*" says Capitano Leo. He picks out
and pays for a little rosary bracelet for Delaney and a
St. Peter medal on a chain for Riley. "Here is something to remind you of your first trip to the Vatican
and this harrowing day."

Dodging a group of tourists taking pictures in
front of the great Basilica, Captiano Leo takes the children to a granite disk on the ground in front of one of
the two giant fountains that sit on either side of the
piazza. "Look at all the giant columns," he says.
"They were designed by a man named Bernini. Stand
here on this disk and see how they all line up!"

"This is cool," says Riley as he and Delaney take
turns standing on the disk. The statues on top of the
columns all line up so that the saints are looking
down at the people in the piazza. But the statues of
Jesus and the Apostles over the Basilica are looking up
and out at them.

"Come back here and look at the columns from

another angle," suggests Capitano Leo as he walks with the children to the farthest end of the piazza. "From here, see how the columns curve around the piazza. They are like arms making a great big hug. The solid arc of the columns symbolizes the Church's embrace of humankind. All are welcome here!"

"What's that big spike?" questions Riley looking at the sky-high spire in the center of the *piazza*.

"That is called an obelisk. It was brought here from Egypt on a big boat in the year 37 AD. I'm told it is over 80 feet high and weighs almost a million pounds. It is believed that the Apostle Peter was put to death by hanging upside down on or near that obelisk," explains Capitano Leo. "When Peter knew he was going to be put to death by crucifixion, he insisted that he be crucified upside down. He didn't believe he was worthy to die in the same manner as Jesus . . . you know, head up on the cross.

"The bones in the tomb, St. Peter's tomb where we just came from, they lack the feet bones. The theory is that Peter's assassins cut off his feet in order to get him off the cross and into the tomb."

"Yikes! They cut off his feet? Poor Peter," exclaims Delaney. The thought of a footless St. Peter makes Delaney shiver.

As they ascend the steps to enter St. Peter's Basilica, the giant bells in the clock tower high above their heads toll the half-hour. *Bong. Bong.* The sound rumbles down into their chests.

CHAPTER EIGHT

ST. PETER'S BASILICA

"How did they get those pictures and all that gold up there?" questions Delaney looking way up into the ceiling of the portico, a big, long, high porch that forms the entry to the basilica. "Giants must live here!"

Her eyes grow large as she looks back and forth from one end of the portico to the other. "There they are!" she says pointing to the great big statues of men on horseback at either ends of the broad portico.

"Those giants are marble statues of Emperors Constantine and Charlemagne. A long time ago they were very involved in allowing Christianity to grow in Europe. Someone believed they belonged in this holy place," says Capitano Leo. "They were great people, but not real giants."

"Giant's doors!" gasps Delaney looking straight ahead.

Facing them are five pair of double doors that reach almost to the ceiling of the portico. The doors look like they are made of metal and each has

something carved into it. Capitano Leo explains that
the pair of doors to the right are the 'Holy Doors' and
are only used during Jubilee years, which happen
every twenty-five years. Standing back and looking
up to see the full height, Delaney and Riley inspect
the pictures carved into some of the doors. The pictures tell stories of the lives of Jesus and the Apostles
Peter and Paul. One set of doors pictorializes the
seven sacraments.

ENTRATA is written on a sign pointing to one of
the open doors. Riley figures that *ENTRATA* must be
Italian for 'entrance'. That's at least three Italian
words he has figured out today.

"Wow! This is the biggest church I have ever
seen," exclaims Riley as they walk through the door.
His eyes open very wide to take in all that lies before
him: the high arching and decorated ceiling, statues of
every shape and size, marble of every color, chapels
and altars with giant candle sticks, and bigger than
life size pictures. He learned about Saint Peter's
Basilica in religion class and has seen it on television -
- but this -- why, it's more grand than he could ever
have imagined.

"Well, yes," says Capitano Leo with a little
chuckle. "It has to be the biggest church you ever saw

"Wow! This is the biggest church I have ever seen."

because it is the largest church in the entire world. In fact six of your American football fields could fit inside St. Peter's Basilica. In here are nearly 500 columns, over 430 large statues, 40 separate altars, and 10 domes. Mass is said nearly all day long here, and confessions are heard in every language.

"This basilica holds a rich history of Christianity - - of Jesus, the Apostles, especially Peter, the Popes, and saints. Peter isn't the only Pope buried here, you know.

"Come, let's walk down the main aisle." The magnificence of the basilica has left Riley and Delaney speechless. They draw very close to Capitano Leo as they head toward an altar with four twisty, turny columns on each corner.

Just then, the phone under Capitano Leo's shirt buzzes. He answers. He frowns. "*Si*, I'm on my way."

"Children, the guards on the *Ufficio* Gate need a hand. Can you stay here for a few minutes? Just wait right here and I'll be back to take you to your aunt. OK?"

"Sure," says Riley. Taking his little sister's hand, they turn and watch the Capitano walk away. The guard's footsteps on the marble floor echo through the huge Basilica. Right now Riley is feeling mighty small and alone.

"Group, right this way," is all that Riley hears before a large group of tourists push their way into the Basilica and stop right where he and Delaney are standing, jostling them nearly off their feet. Riley turns and tries to push the people away, but instead he and Delaney are swept into the crowd.

"Stop right here," the lady leading the group of tourists commands. "Over there is the very famous statue of St. Peter. People like to come here to rub or kiss his foot. See how shiny it is. This statue, and many of the other statues and paintings of the Apostle Peter show him holding keys in his hand. That's how you can tell its Peter. Once Jesus gave him the keys to heaven, Peter wasn't going to let go of them. Go over there and rub his foot and say a prayer that when your time comes, he will use the keys to let you into heaven and not that other place!"

Riley and Delaney are forced to get in line with the pushy tourists. Riley fears getting separated from Delaney, so he just goes with the flow for the time being. Besides, he is curious and would like to see the statue the lady is talking about. When it's their turn to rub the foot of Peter, Riley has to lift Delaney up to reach it.

"Come on Delaney, let's go back and wait for Capitano Leo," says Riley as he pulls his sister free of the group of tourists.

"Wait, let's go see what's up there," says Delaney pointing to the Papal Altar – that's the one with the

"Look up there! There's a man on a rope."

four twisty-turny columns. Riley glances in the
direction of the *ENTRATA* and decides that Capitano
Leo won't be back for a few more minutes.

They take off running toward the altar. The
closer they get to the altar, the bigger it gets!

"Look up there! There's a man on a rope," says
Delaney pointing to a man over 100 feet in the air
with a safety rope tied around his waist. He is sitting
at the top of one of the four twisting, turning columns
that looked so much smaller from the entranceway.

"Oh, he's just doing maintenance," says a man
dressed in blue coveralls with a Vatican emblem on
the front pocket. This workman had noticed the
excitement on the children's faces as they ran toward
the altar. He hopes his English is good enough for
them to understand.

"Every so often the columns need cleaning or
the lights up there need changing. Those columns are
so high and so strong that the men can swing from
one to another if they need to, just like Tarzan in the
movies," says the workman.

"This is the famous altar where the Pope says
Mass. Perhaps you have seen it on television when
Masses are celebrated here at Christmas or Easter time."

"Look up through the columns to the top.
There's a canopy. It's called a *baldacchino*," says the

workman. He points up and the children's eyes follow. "See the dove in the middle? It represents the Holy Spirit."

"It kind of looks like the pigeons we played with outside, only really shiny," observes Delaney cocking her head.

"Now look all the way up above the altar, way up above the columns and the canopy and the dove. See the light coming through the ceiling at the very top. You are looking up through the inside of a dome. This dome happens to be the famous dome that you see from outside and that is known all over the world as being St. Peter's. There are words written in Latin around the inside near the top. Translated to English they say, *You are Peter and Upon this Rock I Will Build My Church and I Will Give You the Keys to Heaven.*"

"Now, directly below that dome, and directly below the Pope's Altar, about twenty meters down, lies the tomb of St. Peter," the workman tells them.

"St. Peter's tomb? We were there this morning!" admits an excited Riley.

The workman gets a puzzled look on his face. Perhaps his English isn't so good after all. These young children would never have been permitted in Peter's tomb.

"There's another picture of a dove at the end of the church," observes an excited Delaney pointing

toward the very end of
the basilica.

"Is that a
giant's chair?"
Delaney asks
seeing what
looks like a
chair float-
ing in gold
and silver
clouds
beneath the
dove. Now
Delaney is
sure that giants
live here.

"That is the very
famous and sacred
'Chair of Peter' or *Cattedra
Petri* in Latin," says the workman.

"Did St. Peter actually sit in that chair?" questions
Riley. "It looks awfully big. How big was Peter?"

"He had to be a giant to live in this church and sit
in that chair," argues Delaney.

"No, he wasn't a giant. Just a normal-sized
person. I don't think that he ever actually sat in that
chair," answers the workman. "It looks to be about ten

feet tall; much too big for an average man to sit in. That big chair more importantly symbolizes that this is the place where the head of the Church belongs. However, a chair that Peter really did sit in is enclosed inside that big bronze chair."

"Can we go see it?" pleads Delaney.

The workman smiles at them as he extends his arm and hand and says, "Go look. Be my guest."

Weaving in and out of the columns, statues and tourists, the children find their way to the dove and chair they saw from the Papal Altar. Only now the dove is way, way up above their heads and much higher up than it looked from back by the altar. The Chair of St. Peter is even bigger!

Out of the corner of his left eye Riley catches a glimpse of a dark figure moving like a shadow in the direction of dove and St. Peter's chair. Riley turns and watches. The dark figure seems to float in and out of the columns and doorways and along the poorly lit edge of the Basilica. At times the figure stops, looks up and down and then over its shoulder, then slinks away. All at once Riley realizes it's the same hooded figure he saw earlier in the Vatican Gardens. He wonders again if this is the Pope's intruder – or is it an evil spirit?! What should he do?

"Delaney, watch that person in the hood and see where he goes. It just might be the Pope's intruder. I want to go find Capitano Leo. You stay here."

Suddenly Riley does not feel comfortable leaving Delaney standing there all alone. What if it is the intruder and he's dangerous? It's just not safe. Besides, she could get lost. Then what would he do? His aunt and parents would really freak-out if his little sister was missing on their first day in a foreign country.

Riley looks on as the hooded figure disappears behind the wall with the dove on it.

Changing his mind, Riley says, "Let's follow him, Delaney. At least we can tell Capitano Leo what we saw, where he went and what he does. Let's be very quiet and tip-toe around the back of that wall."

Quietly the children creep behind the wall and see an open doorway beneath the dove. Riley sneaks up and peaks around the door jam to see if he can see his suspected intruder. Nothing there – he pulls Delaney behind him as his eyes adjust to the darkened room.

"There he is!" whispers Riley. "Look, he's picking up that chalice. Now he's looking inside. Now he's setting it down and picking up a candlestick."

The hooded figure, carrying the candlestick, turns and drifts very slowly deeper into the darkened room. Riley cannot see him anymore, so he and

Delaney get on their knees to crawl a little further into the room. They strain to see in the dark.

Suddenly someone behind them shouts something in Italian. Chills run down Riley's spine as he recalls the fright he had in St. Peter's tomb when Capitano Leo called out to them. He pulls Delaney closer to him and puts his arms around her protectively.

"How in the world did the two of you get back here behind the Chair of St. Peter?"

Riley looks up and is relieved to see the familiar face of Capitano Leo peering at them through the doorway.

"We were following the boogeyman!" says Delaney in a very loud whisper.

Somewhat embarrassed, Riley confesses, "I saw someone sneaking around and I thought it might be the Pope's intruder. We were watching him so I could tell you about him."

Capitano Leo thinks the kids have an overactive imagination. He wonders if they spent too much time in the darkness of Peter's tomb this morning. "We'll try and find him later. Right now I have to get you back to your aunt. You don't want to get me into trouble do you?"

Capitano Leo takes Delaney by the hand and puts his hand on Riley's back. He is not going to let these kids out of his sight again.

*The hooded figure, carrying the candlestick, turns and drifts very slowly
deeper into the darkened room.*

"Let me show you one of my favorite pictures in this basilica,"
says Capitano Leo.

Delaney starts to check out some of the pictures on the walls as they walk toward the exit. "I like these pictures," she offers. "I like to draw pictures too."

"Well then, come over here and let me show you one of my favorite pictures in this basilica," says Capitano Leo.

"There it is," Capitano Leo says pointing to a brightly colored picture above one of the altars. "Why don't you tell me what you see?"

"That man is in the water and he looks really scared," observes Delaney. "So do those men behind him in the boat!"

Riley studies it for a while then asks, "Is that Jesus holding out his hand?"

"Very good!" says Capitano Leo. "That is Jesus. And the scared looking man in the water is St. Peter. The other Apostles are still in the boat. This is a famous picture of when Jesus had invited Peter to walk on the water. When Peter realizes what is happening, he panics and starts to sink. Jesus tells him to 'have faith' and 'do not be afraid.' It teaches us that if we trust God with all our heart, He will take care of us. We have no need to worry.

"This picture and most all of the others here in the Basilica look like paintings, right? Well, they are really mosaics. That means they are made up of thousands of little colored tiles pasted together to make a picture. It is truly amazing. It's like a miracle that the artists who made these could make such beautiful images with tiny pieces of colored stone. They certainly loved God a lot to do this."

Riley can see that Capitano Leo really treasures this place.

"Now, let's get going," says Capitano Leo. "It's high time that I returned you to the Holy Father and Sister Philomena."

Riley cringes at the thought of coming face to face with the Pope and his aunt. How mad are they going to be that Delaney and he went into St. Peter's tomb?

Good grief, how bad is it to have the Pope mad at you?

"Who is that white lady and who is she holding?" questions Delaney struggling to keep up and to look at all the art at the same time.

"That is the very famous *Pieta*," explains Capitano Leo. "It is so beautiful. So graceful. It is a marble carving of the Blessed Mother holding the body of her son, Jesus, as He is taken down from the Cross. The famous artist, Michelangelo, made it. Oh children, you have so much to see and learn about this place. I hope you can come back here and spend more time."

"Me too," says Riley. "Thank you, Capitano Leo, for showing us around. This place is really neat. But that tomb – I think I'll stay away from there."

Before exiting the basilica they stop at the holy water font to bless themselves. Statues of cherubs more than twice the size of Delaney hold up a giant clamshell filled with holy water. Again, Riley has to pick up Delaney so that she can dip her little fingers in the holy water to bless herself.

CHAPTER NINE

PIZZA WITH THE POPE

Riley's body feels heavy like it's filled with sand as he, Delaney and Capitano Leo climb the tall and never-ending staircase to get back to the Pope's apartment. Riley is afraid to face his aunt and the Pope again. What will be the punishment for crawling into St. Peter's tomb?

"Tarsus!" shouts Delaney as she sees the white cat she was following when she and Riley fell into the hole in the ground. "You found Tarsus!" she exclaims as she runs into the room where her aunt and the Pope are meeting. She kneels down and scoops the cat into her arms.

"I see you have met my cat," says the Pope. "How naughty of him to lead you to the hole that leads to the tomb of St. Peter. I thought only Tarsus could get in that way. You children surprise me!"

Riley decides then and there that it is best to confess and say he's sorry right away and get on with the punishment, whatever it may be. "Your Holiness, I apologize for going into St. Peter's tomb without

permission. We really didn't mean to do it," admits Riley. "Forgive Delaney and me."

"I appreciate your apology, Riley," says the Pope. "Capitano Leo has explained it to me and I understand it was an accident. None of us are used to having children around and it's been a long time since we were children ourselves. We forget how quickly you can get into mischief."

Riley looks up to Capitano Leo with a high degree of admiration. Capitano Leo winks at him as if to say, you're doing the right thing. "Thank you Holy Father," is all Riley can think to say. It's the right thing to say.

"Tell me, did you look at the bones of St. Peter?" asks the Pope with a strange hint of curiosity.

"No! I only shook the box," admits Riley. "Why, is it a sin or something if you touch them?"

"Oh no," responds the Pope emphatically. "That would not be a sin."

"Would you like to see the relics I have of St. Peter? I have a special silver box, called a reliquary, that holds some of St. Peter's bones. We Pope's like to keep them near us so we remember from whence we came and to where we are going. Follow me to my private chapel and I will show you," says the Pope.

His Holiness turns and leads the band of four down the hall to his very own chapel.

Sister Philomena removes the cat from Delaney's lap and takes the little girl and Riley by their hands. She feels her heart pounding as they walk down the hallway. This is such a special and generous offer of the Holy Father. As far as she knows, rarely has anyone outside the papal household been allowed into the Pope's very own private chapel. Certainly she knows that no outsiders have ever been allowed to view the relics of St. Peter.

Once inside the chapel, Sister Philomena, Riley, Delaney and Capitano Leo kneel and quietly say a prayer. The Pope approaches the altar and retrieves a silver box. He motions them to come up and look into the box.

"See, it's just bones," says the Holy Father. "Two thousand year old bones. But they are his bones, St. Peter's. He is the man who Jesus selected as His first Apostle and the one He picked as the first leader of His Church. They are indeed sacred and holy."

As Riley looks at the relics a feeling comes over him. For the first time he realizes that Peter was in fact a real person. He looks to the Pope and says, "Before now St. Peter was someone I read about in a book. He seemed like a make-believe character. But hearing you talk about his life, then finding his tomb,

and now looking at his bones, I believe in him. Saint Peter really did live and he really was a friend of Jesus Christ wasn't he?"

"Yes Riley," says the Holy Father. "Peter was very real and so was Jesus. In his writings Peter tells us to live righteous lives. That means to live our lives as God wants us to – put God above everything, love our neighbor, and always do what is right even though it may not be popular. If we do this, then we too will live with Jesus in our hearts and one day in heaven."

As they leave the private chapel the Pope asks, "Sister Philomena, do you and the children have time to

have lunch with me? Our business is concluded
for today and you are free to leave, but I bet these
children would like something to eat."

"That would be most generous, your Holiness.
We probably have missed lunch at the convent. What
do you say children?"

"Sure," says Riley. His stomach is churning after
the events of this morning, and he is hungry. But
more importantly, the very idea of spending more
time with the Pope and learning more about his aunt's
work with him is something he cannot pass up.
Never in a billion years would his friends back home
believe that he hung out with the Pope! How has his
aunt kept this secret?

"I'm going to go play with Tarsus," says Delaney
as she spots the big white cat and takes off running
after it.

"Did you figure out who the Vatican intruder
is?" asks Riley. "When we were in the tomb I was
afraid the shadow I saw was your intruder. I was
really scared."

"I bet you were scared," says a sympathetic
Sister Philomena. "What a frightful way to begin your
visit."

"The shadow turned out to be Capitano Leo, and
he's our friend now."

"But I also saw this hooded guy in the garden and again in the basilica, by the dove and Peter's Chair. Something made me think he's the intruder. He did some weird things. But then Capitano Leo found us and brought us back here."

"Sounds interesting," says Sister Philomena. "Holy Father is it OK to tell Riley what we have found, or have not found so far?"

"Certainly. He seems like a smart, inquisitive and trustworthy boy," says the Holy Father.

"The Holy Father and I did make a list of potential intruders. Short of it being a ghost of a past Pope, which it isn't," she laughs, "we think we have a reasonable suspect. We considered several possibilities, including an employee, a Swiss Guard and a Vatican Museum worker before we came up with what we think is the answer.

"We ruled out the idea of an employee because they are always accounted for when they clock-in for work and clock-out before going home. The intruder is here at all different hours of the day and night. The Pope is sure that the intruder has been sneaking around late at night after all the employees have left for the day.

"It could not possibly be a Swiss Guard. They are all much too loyal. Besides, Capitano Leo keeps excellent watch over their activities. Many are planning on studying for the priesthood when their guard duty is over.

"The possibility of a Vatican Museum worker was also considered. We thought perhaps someone was sneaking in here to view the art in the apartment. But that just didn't make any sense. Museum people can visit this artwork whenever they want. All they have to do is ask. Why would they sneak around?

"That left us one possibility and we are going to watch him. Monsignor DiGiulio is quite elderly and sadly is a bit senile. He wanders around a lot. Most of the time he is dressed in black and puts a hood over his head for warmth. He likes to walk around on the marble floors in his stocking feet. He's a quiet, innocent and harmless man. At one time he was the personal secretary for an earlier Pope, so he is familiar with the Vatican and all its secret places. To keep track of his whereabouts, the Pope has agreed to let us put a bell on the bottom of his cassock. We'll just wait and see."

"Lunch is ready," announces Sister Mary John, a pleasant looking nun dressed in a white habit and wearing an apron.

A delightful smell fills Riley's nose as they enter the dining room. Riley's mouth begins to water and he cannot believe what he sees.

It's pizza! The Pope is serving pizza!

"It's one of my favorites," says the Pope as he watches Riley and Delaney's eyes light up.

"Mine too," says Delaney. She climbs up onto a large dining room chair and struggles to put Tarsus on the chair next to her. The cat complies. However, Sister Philomena, horrified by the actions of the little girl, begins to remove the cat.

"NO!" bellows Delaney.

"It's all right, Sister. The cat can stay," says the benevolent Pope.

Capitano Leo has to excuse himself from the lunch. "Duty calls. I have to prepare for the dignitaries that are scheduled to meet with the Pope this afternoon. Enjoy your lunch and I hope to see you all again soon."

Sister Philomena relaxes and lets out a big sigh of relief. How will she ever survive a summer with these children?

As Capitano Leo leaves, Riley wonders just exactly what he meant when he said 'Sister Philomena will provide you with lots of adventure this summer.'

"It's all right, Sister. The cat can stay," says the benevolent Pope.

PETER'S BONES ARE MISSING!

T he Pope and his guests have just finished eating the most delicious thin crust pizza ever made. The meal was topped off with a kind of ice cream that the Pope calls *gelato*. Delaney had two servings and Riley had three.

"Holy Father, something terrible has happened!" shouts Capitano Leo as he bursts into the dining room.

"What is it, Capitano Leo?" asks the Pope. "You look like you have seen the devil."

"Worse! But I'm sure it's the devil's work," says a breathless Capitano Leo.

"I went back to secure your private chapel before the afternoon visitors arrive. I wanted to see the relics of St. Peter one more time. When I looked, they were gone. The silver reliquary, the bones, all of it!"

"No! That cannot be," exclaims the Pope. "Sister Philomena, Capitano Leo, please help me!"

Sister Philomena pulls a cell phone out of the pocket of her habit and starts to give orders to whomever is on the other end.

Capitano Leo, on his cell phone, is telling someone to "secure the Apostolic Palace."

Riley and Delaney look on in horror, excitement and amazement.

Riley realizes he needs to get Delaney out of the way while their aunt and Capitano Leo get to work on the investigation. Thinking she'll be safe and out of the way in the foyer to the Pope's apartment, he takes her there to play with Tarsus. After being lost so many times already today, it's a sure bet that she will not go very far without him.

It's not long before Sister Philomena and Capitano Leo deduce that only members of the Papal household and the afternoon's visitors were in the Apostolic Palace between the time the Pope showed them Peter's bones and the time that Capitano Leo found them missing.

"It's an inside job," speculates Riley.

Perhaps to humor him, but maybe to test him, his aunt asks, "Why do you say that, Sherlock? Why don't you think it is one of the visitors here to see the Pope?"

"Because, if I were coming to meet with the Pope and wanted to steal something, I would steal it on the way out, not on the way in. If I took it before I met the Pope, he would see it! If I took it on the way out,

94

I could just run with it!"

"Riley, I like your thinking," says Sister
Philomena. "Besides, what you don't know is that
people coming to see the Pope are asked to leave all
their personal items in an adjoining office before
meeting him. The Swiss Guards tell them that their
items are subject to search. It's a little precaution. So,
I agree with you. It's an inside job.

"Capitano Leo has many of the members of the
Papal household gathered in a room downstairs. He
is going to be interviewing them. It might be good
experience for you to watch and listen to how he con-
ducts the interviews," says Sister Philomena.

Riley feels so privileged. He could never have
imagined his 'boring summer with a bunch of nuns'
would provide this adventure.

Just then, Delaney lets out a blood-curdling
scream. She begins shouting, "It's the boogeyman!
Help! It's the boogeyman! Riley, help me! Aunt
Philomena, save me!"

Riley, Sister Philomena and the Pope rush to the
foyer where Delaney has been playing with Tarsus.
The little girl is crouched in the corner holding onto
the cat for dear life. She is screaming and sobbing
hysterically.

Standing over her is a dark clad figure with a

hood over his head. His cold blank stare is focused on Delaney. He's reaching out with the boney first finger of his left hand pointing right at her. His other hand is holding a candlestick. It looks like the candlestick is cocked above Delaney's head ready to deliver a blow. A silver box that looks like the reliquary is tucked under his arm.

Riley rushes in and pulls Delaney away from the man's stare. Riley becomes a human shield, standing between Delaney and the 'boogeyman.'

Sister Philomena realizes that the box tucked under the hooded figure's arm is in fact the reliquary that contains Peter's bones.

"It's the thief! Don't move!" she orders. The boogeyman looks around to see who is talking. He looks confused.

She pulls the children to her protectively, then reaches for her cell phone. She calls Capitano Leo and the Guards to come and help them.

"It's the intruder!" shouts Riley as he realizes this is the same dark figure that he saw in the Vatican Gardens and in the basilica. "We saw him take that candlestick from the basilica."

From behind them, they hear the Pope, in a kind, calm voice, say, "Monsignor DiGiulio, what do

Standing over her is a dark clad figure with a hood over his head.

we have here?" He approaches the dark figure, the so-called boogeyman, and takes the reliquary and candlestick away from him.

"Now Monsignor, you know you are not supposed to go around picking up things like this. Why don't you go see Sister Mary John in the kitchen? I am sure she has some lunch for you."

The dark figure looks up at the Pope and, pulling the hood from his head, smiles and says, "Thank you. I think I would like that." Without his hood the Monsignor looks like a very pleasant, white-haired, grandfatherly man, but a man who has grown confused and forgetful with age.

Monsignor DiGiulio turns and smiles at Riley and Delaney. "What lovely children. Haven't I seen you before?" he asks. He no longer looks like a boogeyman as he turns and shuffles off toward the kitchen. Riley can see that

98

he is in his stocking feet.

Puzzled, Riley and Delaney look to the Pope and their aunt and the Capitano for answers.

"I think we just solved two of our so-called mysteries," says Sister Philomena. "Monsignor DiGiulio has to be the intruder. He's been living in the Vatican for a very long time. He not only knows every inch of the Vatican and this Apostolic Palace, he probably even has keys to places that nobody else knows about.

"Unfortunately, when elderly people like him become senile they wander about at all hours of the day and night. It's like they are looking for something but cannot quite remember what.

"Monsignor DiGiulio has to be the thief, too. After all, we caught him with the reliquary in his hand. I imagine he saw the box out of place, picked it up to put it away, and then forgot he had it in his hand and walked off with it. He's just old and forgetful. God bless him!"

"Good job, all of you," says the Pope. "Capitano Leo, if you please, come with me. I want to return the reliquary and Peter's bones to my private chapel. Then, if you don't mind, I'll excuse myself. I have visitors waiting.

"Sister Philomena, my driver is waiting to drive you and the children back to Grottaferrata. I loved meeting you, Riley and Delaney. I am sure we will be seeing more of each other this summer."

Leaving the room, the Pope turns and says, "Sister Philomena, let's forget about putting the bells on Monsignor DiGiulio. Now that I know it's him, I'll consider him to be the official Papal intruder."

"I must go and dismiss the employees," says Capitano Leo. "I will explain what has happened and ask if they will just keep an eye out for Monsignor DiGiulio. He's really a sweet and gentle man.

"Signore Riley and Signorina Delaney, I enjoyed rescuing you," he teases. "I hope to be able to show you more of the Vatican on another day."

"So, how did you like your first day in Italy?" Sister Philomena asks.

Smiling a smile of accomplishment, Riley says, "I think I'll stay another day, if you don't mind!"

They all laugh, and hand-in-hand Sister Philomena, Riley and Delaney turn and head for the marble staircase to go down to their waiting car.

Delaney turns and waves 'good-bye' to Tarsus, who is sitting regally on the top step.

THE END

Don't Miss the Next
ADVENTURE!

Adventures
with
Sister Philomena
Special Agent for
The Pope

BREAK-IN

AT THE BASILICA

Written By Dianne Ahern

Illustrated By Katherine Larson

The following is an excerpt from Book Two in the series of

Adventures With Sister Philomena, Special Agent to the Pope

The small man in shabby gray coat and trousers tries to make himself as small as possible as he squeezes between the clumsy looking wooden choir chairs. It is nightfall and Luigi has come to the Basilica of St. Francis in Assisi with the intent to steal something of great value.

Luigi is a desperate and poor man. He has no money. His only daughter, whom he loves very much, wants to become a nun and Luigi wants her to have a dowry to take to the convent when she enters. He is afraid she will be refused entry into the Order unless he can offer the sisters some money or an object of value. God forbid his daughter will have to live forever poor like him.

Several weeks ago he came to the grand Basilica of Saint Francis to pray for an answer to his dilemma. It was then that he discovered a beautiful silver stand tucked away in a display case in a small room near the main altar. At the time he thought this silver thing would be perfect. The more he thought about it, the more certain he became. The stand looks very special and very beautiful, just like his daughter is special and beautiful. It must be quite valuable because it is in this the most famous Basilica in the whole world. Then he wondered: Why is it tucked away in a small room like this? If I take it, will anyone ever know it's gone?

Luigi tries not to breathe. "I will hide here until the guards leave."

Just then, a young man in a black uniform walks past his hideaway. "Hah! He does not see me here in this dark corner!"

"These young men, these guards, they love their uniforms and the power they think it gives them," Luigi scoffs to himself. Then he thinks about all the money they are paid for doing not much more than telling the tourists to be silent. *'Silence'* they shout every few minutes when the tourists get too excited about the beautiful church. Then at closing the guards strut through the basilica just to be sure all the tourists are gone. He knows this because he has watched their actions for the last two weeks as he planned his robbery.

It's at least an hour after the guards leave before Luigi decides to move from his cramped position between the enormous dark wooden chairs. While he was waiting he ate the small sandwich he brought with him and washed it down with cheap wine from a little cardboard box. The bread, although crumbly, was sweet and a perfect compliment to the salty cheese in his sandwich. Luigi is careful to eat over the opening in his sack so he doesn't leave any crumbs behind on the floor. "Yes sir, I am a cautious thief," he thinks.

Suddenly a chill runs down his spine. The sunlight that hours ago lit up the stained glass windows high above his head has long vanished. Now, the light from the full moon casts strange shadows on the pictures paint-ed on the walls of the basilica. His skin turns all prickly.

"Maybe this isn't such a good idea," he murmurs to himself. But it is too late to turn back.

He pulls a heavy flashlight out of his rucksack. "This should do the job," he whispers as he slaps the palm of his hand with the handle of the flashlight. *Whap, whap!*

Quietly and carefully, he crawls out from between the wooden choir chairs, pulling the empty sack behind him. Using his flashlight, Luigi searches for and finds the stairs that lead to the lower part of the basilica. Although it is summer, the coldness and dampness from the stone steps and floor creep into his joints and he feels an ache in his bones.

The light from Luigi's flashlight dances over the arched ceiling and walls of the lower basilica. As he searches for the door that will lead him to his treasure, his light passes over the images that adorn the walls – pictures of angels, saints, apostles and, yes, of Jesus. He can feel them watching him!

"Oh, forgive me you holy ones," he prays out loud. "If you knew how desperate I am for something of value, you would not condemn me."

Just as he is about to enter the room where his treasure awaits him, his light strikes a painting with images of grotesque looking people being pulled down to hell. "Oh, Dio mio, please do not sent me to hell for this. I do love You dear Lord. But this is for my daughter, "he pleads in the empty, almost tomb-like basilica. ...More...

Look for "Break-In at the Basilica" at your local book seller
for the rest of the adventure

Italian
Words
and
Phrases

Whenever we travel to foreign places, it is nice to be able to converse with people in their own language. Even if we only can only speak a few words of their language, that alone lets our world neighbors know that we care about them and want to get to know them. Here are a few words and phrases that were used in this book and that Riley and Delaney might have learned in this adventure.

Italian Word	**English Meaning**
Basilica	Basilica - A big church built according to a specific architectural design that forms a cross
Buon giorno	Good morning or good day
Buona notte	Good night
Carabiniere	The army police who maintain order
Cattedra	Chair or throne
Certamente	Certainly or sure
Chiesa	Church
Ciao	Hello or Goodbye
Come si dice?	How do you say?
Dio misericordioso	Merciful God or Lord have mercy (said as a prayer)
Entrata / Uscita	Entrance / Exit
Fratello	Brother
Gelato	Italian ice cream
Giardino	Garden
Grazie	Thank you
Hai capito?	Do you understand?
Il Papa	The Pope
Mangiare	Eat
Oh, Dio mio	Oh, my God (said as a prayer)
Padre / Madre	Father / Mother
Piazza	Public square or cental point in the neighborhood or city
Polizia	The civil police who investigate crimes
San Pietro	Saint Peter
Scavi	Diggings or tomb
Sì	Yes
Signora/Signorina	Madam or Mrs. / Miss or young lady
Signore	Sir or mister
Sorella	Sister
Vaticano	Vatican
Vincoli	Chains
Vino	Wine
Zia / Zio	Aunt / Uncle

Colore (Color):

Italian ...	English
Rosso	Red
Nero	Black
Giallo	Yellow
Verde	Green
Aracione	Orange
Marrone	Brown
Porpora	Purple
Grigio	Grey
Blu	Blue
Rosa	Rose

Frutta (Fruit)
& Verdura (Vegetable):

Italian ...	English
Mela	Apple
Arancia	Orange
Banana	Banana
Pompelmo	Grapefruit
Uva	Grapes
Fagiolo	Bean
Pomodoro	Tomato
Cetriolo	Cucumber
Pera	Pear
Carota	Carrot

Contare da 1 a 10
(Count 1 to 10):

Italian ...	English
uno	one
due	two
tre	three
quattro	four
cinque	five
sei	six
sette	seven
otto	eight
nove	nine
dieci	ten

Giorno della settimana
(Day of the week):

Italian ...	English
lunedi	Monday
martedi	Tuesday
mercoledi	Wednesday
giovedi	Thursday
venerdi	Friday
sabato	Saturday
domenica	Sunday
oggi	Today
domani	Tomorrow
ieri	Yesterday